Apple Cake

A RECIPE FOR LOVE

JULIE PASCHKIS

HARCOURT CHILDREN'S BOOKS
Houghton Mifflin Harcourt
Boston   New York   2012

Harcourt Children's Books
is an imprint of Houghton Mifflin Harcourt Publishing Company.

www.hmhbooks.com

The illustrations in this book were done in Winsor & Newton gouache
and Koh-I-Noor ink on Arches Aquarelle hot press watercolor paper.
The text type was set in 18 pt. Clichee.
The display type was set in Chic Hand Bold.

LIBRARY OF CONGRESS CATALOGING-IN-PUBLICATION DATA

Paschkis, Julie.
Apple cake : a recipe for love / written by Julie Paschkis.
p. cm.
Summary: Ida always has her nose in a book and Alfonso
is unable to get her attention until he bakes a very special
apple cake for her. Includes cake recipe.
ISBN 978-0-547-80745-4
[1. Love—Fiction. 2. Cake—Fiction. 3. Cooking (Apples)—Fiction.]
I. Title.
PZ7.P2686App 2012
[E]—dc23   2011041930

Manufactured in China
LEO 10 9 8 7 6 5 4 3 2 1

4500355325

To J.M.E.

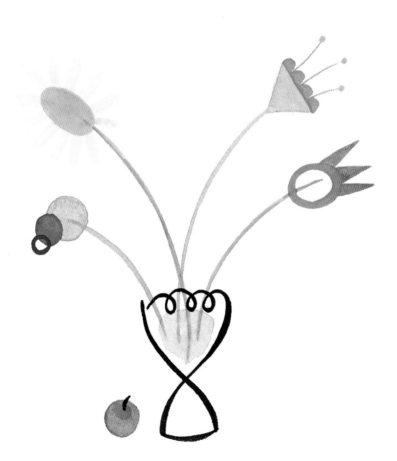

Beautiful, kind, brilliant Ida . . .

always kept her nose in a book.

What could be more interesting than her book?

Ida never looked up, no matter what Alfonso did.

So he decided to bake her a cake.

First he took three apples:

one green and two red.

He peeled the apples, cut them up,

and set them in water while he made the batter.

In a new bowl, he beat
two tablespoons of butter

with a cup of sugar.

He took an egg

and added it to the bowl.

He sifted in a cup of flour
and a teaspoon
of baking powder
to make it rise.

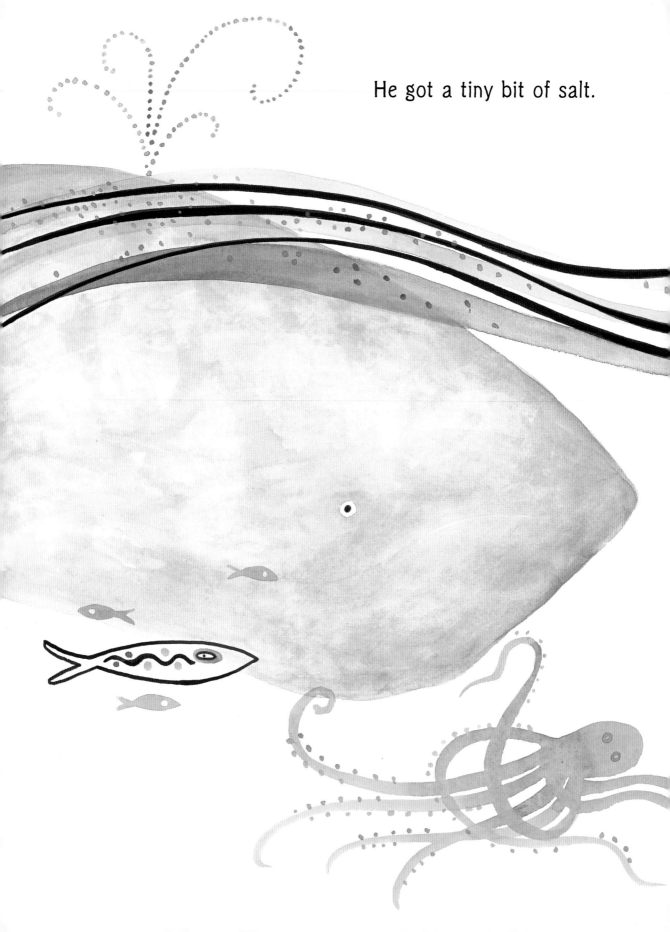

He got a tiny bit of salt.

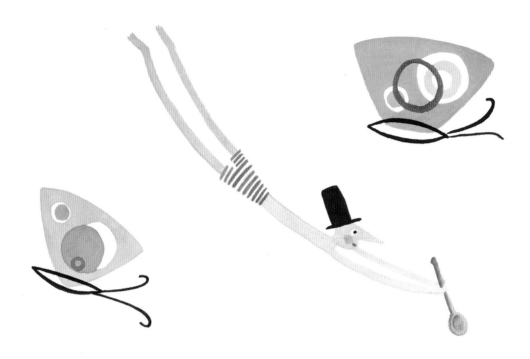

He stirred the apples and the batter together.

He stirred in three wishes: one bitter

and two sweet.

He sprinkled the cake
with cinnamon and sugar
and baked it.

Ida smelled something delicious.
She peeked.
She put down her book.

Alfonso handed her the apple cake.

Ida looked right at Alfonso.
She smiled. He smiled.

And together they ate it all up.

APPLE CAKE

This is the recipe that Alfonso knows by heart. It came from Julie's great-grandmother, Lily Jane Powell. It makes 8 servings.

For the cake:
3 small apples
2 tablespoons butter, at room temperature
1 cup sugar
1 large egg
1 cup flour
1 teaspoon baking powder
1/8 teaspoon salt

For the topping:
2 tablespoons sugar
2 teaspoons cinnamon

Grease a 9-inch by 9-inch square or a 9-inch round baking pan with butter. Preheat the oven to 350 degrees.

Peel the apples and remove the core and seeds. Cut them into pieces that are about 3/4-inch big, and put them in cold water.

In a large bowl, beat the softened butter and sugar together until creamy. Add the egg and beat until the egg is completely mixed in.

In another bowl, sift together the flour, baking powder, and salt. Add the flour mixture to the batter and mix well. The batter will be quite stiff.

Shake some of the water off the apples and gently mix them into the batter.

Put the batter into the greased baking pan and spread it evenly.

In a small bowl, mix together the 2 tablespoons sugar and 2 teaspoons cinnamon. Sprinkle the cinnamon sugar over the cake.

Bake the cake until it pulls away from the edges of the pan and the top looks golden brown and flaky, about 55 to 60 minutes. The cake will be soft and moist, almost like pudding, and the cinnamon sugar will be a crispy layer on the top.

Let the cake cool for 10 minutes in the baking pan. Eat it warm or at room temperature. It is good plain or with whipped cream or vanilla ice cream. It is also a good breakfast cake.